D1146315

THE GREAT ZOO HUNT

Pippa Unwin

M

MACMILLAN CHILDREN'S BOOKS

First published 1989 by
MACMILLAN CHILDREN'S BOOKS
A division of Macmillan Publishers Limited
London and Basingstoke
Associated companies throughout the world

Here is a small town by the sea. In the town there is a zoo. Can you see it?

This is a story about that zoo and the new keeper who nearly got into trouble.

If you look at the pictures carefully you can help him to put things right.

This is the zoo.

Yesterday the new keeper started work.

Can you see him feeding the dolphins and the penguins?

At the end of the day, the new keeper had to feed the
animals and make sure they were all safe inside their
cages.

He gave them their food and he thought he had locked all the doors and gates, but the next day, when he got to work . . .

...he found ten of the animals were missing!

"Oh dear!" he said. "They've escaped! Where are the camel and the elephant? Where have the giraffe, the hippo and the lion gone? And I can't see the monkey, the parrot and snake – or the tiger and zebra."

Can *you* help the keeper find them?

Perhaps one of the animals is hiding in the market place.

Can you see one of the animals in this street?

Who is sleeping in the town square?

Perhaps one of the animals is here.

Can you help the keeper find it?

Is an animal hiding among the houses?

Lots of people are enjoying themselves in the park.

Is one of the animals there too?

What is hiding at the swimming pool?

Is there an animal in the gardens?

Will the keeper find an animal at the beach?

Just one more animal to find!

The keeper is very pleased.

He has all the animals now.

parrot

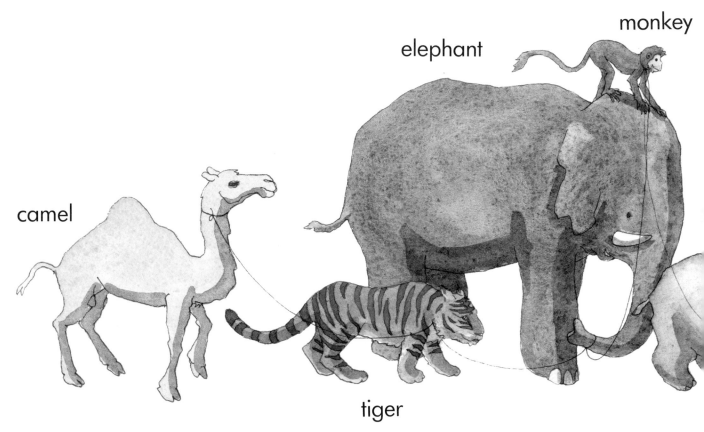

monkey

elephant

camel

tiger

Did you help him to find each of them?

There is just enough time to put them all back in the zoo before it opens.

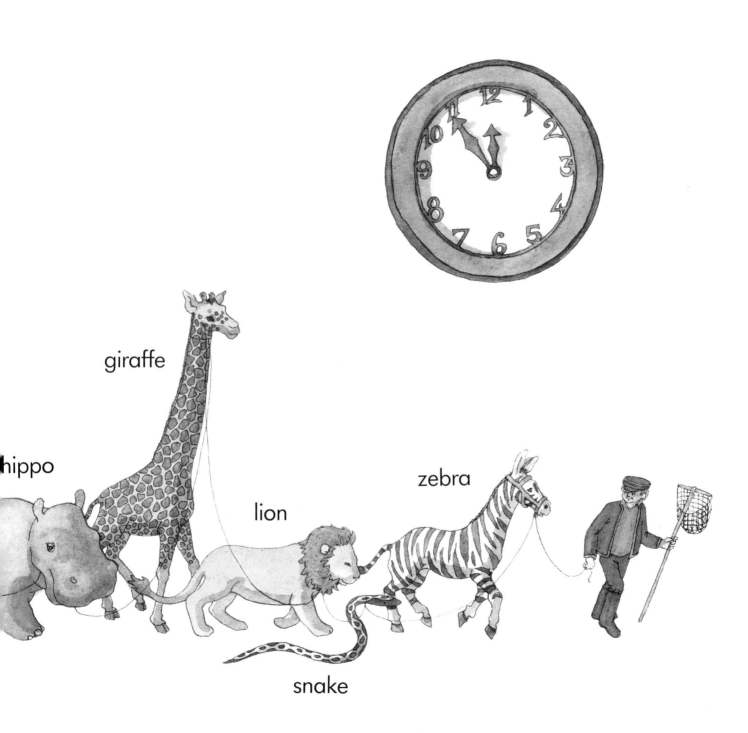

giraffe

hippo

zebra

lion

snake

Now all the animals are safely back.

"Thank you very much for helping me," says the keeper.
"I'd never have found them on my own."

A New Hunt

Now that all the animals are safely back in the zoo, turn back to the beginning of the book to the picture of the whole town. The dotted line shows the route which the keeper took.

If you look again through the other pictures, you will find some of the things the keeper saw while he was searching for the animals – and some that he didn't!

For instance, on page 4 can you see the children riding on the elephant?

Turn to page 10 and see if you can find the dog which is stealing the sausages. And where is the boy who is giving flowers to his girl friend?

In the school playground, the children are playing lots of different games. How many can you spot?

In one picture you can see the sheep escaping. Can you find them being rounded up in another picture?

What does the postman ride on when he is delivering letters?

The window cleaner is also in most of the pictures. Can you find him helping to rescue a cat?

If you follow the keeper on his search, there are more things to look out for in the pictures –I hope you have fun finding them!

Pippa Unwin